STORIES ABOUT NOT BEING AFRAID OF GHOSTS

Compiled by
the Institute of Literature of the Chinese
Academy of Social Sciences

WILDSIDE PRESS

www.wildsidepress.com

Translated by
YANG HSIEN-YI AND GLADYS YANG

Illustrated by
CHENG SHIH-FA

Front cover: Chung Kuei, a famous
figure in Chinese folklore known
for his skill in catching ghosts

Publisher's Note

This is a selection of stories from the first Chinese edition of *Stories About Not Being Afraid of Ghosts* published by the People's Literature Publishing House, Peking, in February 1961. A preface written for the Chinese edition by Ho Chi-fang (1912-1977), Director of the Institute of Literature of the Chinese Academy of Social Sciences, is also included.

Contents

Preface

Ho Chi-fang

There are no ghosts. Belief in ghosts is a backward idea, a superstition and a sign of cowardice. This is a matter of common sense today among the people.

In the past, however, people took a different view. Many believed in ghosts and were afraid of them. There is nothing strange about this. When man was not yet able to comprehend natural and social phenomena in the light of science, he inevitably had all sorts of superstitions. The more so because the reactionary ruling classes fooled and frightened the people with ghosts and gods so as to strengthen their rule.

What should amaze us today is not that there were so many believers in ghosts in those days but that, at a time when believers in ghosts had the upper hand, there was a minority who denied the existence of ghosts. Confucius, as recorded in the *Analects*, had doubts and reservations about ghosts and gods. Hsun Tzu, in "The Removal of Prejudice," ridiculed a "stupid and timid" man who believed in ghosts and goblins. Huan Tan and Wang Chung of the Han Dynasty (206 B.C.-220 A.D.), Juan Chan and Juan Hsiu of the Tsin Dynasty (265-420 A.D.) and Fan Chen of the Southern and Northern Dynasties

1

(420-589 A.D.) all held materialist views. They contended that a man's spirit died with his body or openly maintained that there were no ghosts. Like an eternal fire, disbelief in ghosts or gods has never been stamped out throughout China's history. This has been a never-fading light of our nation's wisdom. We cannot fail to admire the intellectual courage and the brilliance of the ideas of those men of ancient times who refused to be fettered by superstitions about ghosts and gods.

Many ancient Chinese authors of tales and sketches liked writing about ghosts. This often showed, of course, that they were still unable to rise above a superstitious belief in ghosts. But there were some among them who, though admitting the existence of ghosts, had no respect for the ghosts everyone else feared. They held that ghosts were nothing to be afraid of, and they described men who dared to curse, expel, beat or capture ghosts. Such stories are full of meaning. They were ingenious reflections of the dauntless spirit of our people in ancient times. Such are the *Stories About Not Being Afraid of Ghosts* which we have compiled.

In compiling this booklet our aim was not to use these stories to illustrate the materialist ideas of ancient China. Our intention was mainly to present these stories as fables and satires to readers. A man who is cowardly at heart and has not emancipated his mind will be afraid of non-existent ghosts and gods. But if he raises his level of political understanding, does away with superstition and emancipates his mind, he will find not only that ghosts and gods are nothing to be afraid of but that imperialism, reaction, revisionism and all natural or man-made calamities that actually exist, are also nothing

2

for Marxist-Leninists to be afraid of but are something that can be defeated or overcome.

It was after *Renmin Ribao* (*People's Daily*) published "Comrade Mao Tsetung on 'Imperialism and All Reactionaries Are Paper Tigers' " that we started compiling this booklet. Comrade Mao Tsetung said:

All reactionaries are paper tigers. In appearance, the reactionaries are terrifying, but in reality they are not so powerful. From a long-term point of view, it is not the reactionaries but the people who are really powerful.[1]

He said this in a talk with the American journalist Anna Louise Strong in Yenan in 1946. Since then, we have defeated Chiang Kai-shek backed by U.S. imperialism, and founded the People's Republic of China. In the war to resist U.S. aggression and aid Korea, we fought shoulder to shoulder with the Korean people and defeated the aggressive forces of U.S. imperialism. Many facts have borne out Comrade Mao Tsetung's thesis. But how to assess the forces of revolution and the forces of reaction is still a big question, in China and throughout the world, which many people have not yet solved. These people still harbour superstitions; they have still not emancipated, or have not completely emancipated, their minds. They do not understand that the apparent "power" and "strength" of imperialism and all reactionaries at certain times is, historically speaking, merely a transient phenomenon, a factor playing only a temporary role. But their anti-popular character and the fact that

---

[1] "Talk with the American Correspondent Anna Louise Strong," *Selected Works of Mao Tsetung*, Foreign Languages Press, Peking, 1961, Vol. IV, p. 100.

they are already rotten and have no future is the essence of the matter and is a factor playing a constant role. In contrast to the case of the reactionary forces, the apparently insufficient strength of the revolutionary forces at certain times is merely a transient phenomenon, a factor playing only a temporary role; their progressive character and the fact that they enjoy the support of the people and are bound to triumph is the essence of the matter and is a factor playing a constant role. We have every reason, therefore, to despise imperialism and all reactionaries, and we have every assurance and full confidence that we can defeat them. The ghosts described in the tales, like paper tigers, are frightful in appearance. But many ghost-defying stories show that, in reality, there is nothing frightful about them. All these stories make this point: if only man has no fear of ghosts but dares to despise and strike at·them, the ghosts will fear man. "Don't be afraid of ghosts" — not only can this serve us as a simile for strategically despising imperialism and all reactionaries but its content can be broadened to mean: if we are unable to make an end of superstition and emancipate our minds, and are fearful and apprehensive about everything that appears to be frightful but actually isn't so, we can be called "ghost-fearing" and will be as ridiculous as if we were actually afraid of ghosts.

There are no ghosts such as are described in the old stories, but there are actually many things in this world which are like ghosts. Some are big, such as international imperialism and its henchmen in various countries, modern revisionism, serious natural calamities and certain not-yet-reformed members of the landlord and bourgeois classes who have usurped leadership in some organizations at the primary level and staged a come-back there. Some are small, such as difficulties and setbacks in ordinary work, etc. All these can be said to be ghost-like things. Imperialism, reaction, revisionism and so on differ from ghosts in that they really exist while ghosts do not. But they have something in common with the ghosts in the tales: They are always up to deviltry, they always create disturbance and make trouble. Some-times they are ferociously vicious, with hideous features; at other times they take on enchanting guises to bewitch people; they all know how to mask themselves, how to fascinate or terrify people, and their ability to transform and metamorphose themselves puts the ghosts in the old stories completely in the shade. But the most important thing is that, like the ghosts in the tales, they appear frightful but actually are not. Some people fear them and this, just as with fear of ghosts, is due to their backward thinking, to their failure to emancipate their minds and to do away with superstition and to their cowardice stemming from the fact that their subjective understanding does not conform to objective reality. To make a clean sweep of such backward "ghost-fearing" ideas is a serious fighting task for every revolutionary. There are people of another kind who are "half-man-half-ghost." If they are not remoulded into complete human beings, they are likely to turn into complete "ghosts." While they are still "half-man-half-ghost," their reactionary aspect will play the devil and stir up trouble like all the rest of the "ghost" species. It will do a lot of good for people to read the old stories about not being afraid of ghosts and for everyone to promote the spirit of not being afraid of ghosts.

Thoroughgoing dialectical materialists and genuine

proletarian revolutionaries are, of course, much wiser than those people who did not fear ghosts in the old tales. They know perfectly well that the forces of reaction at home or abroad, however powerful they may appear to be, cannot after all stop the mighty and irresistible advancing wheel of history. It is the law of history and of actual life that good will triumph over evil, truth over falsehood, virtue over vice, beauty over ugliness, the new-born revolutionary forces over the decadent reactionary forces, the exploited and oppressed people over the exploiters and the oppressors, and the progressive over the conservative. Therefore, as thoroughgoing dialectical materialists and genuine proletarian revolutionaries see it, there is nothing to be afraid of in this world. Imperialism, reaction, revisionism, the overthrown classes which stage or attempt to stage a come-back, exceptionally severe natural calamities, difficulties and setbacks in ordinary work and struggle, etc. — none of these are to be feared. Strategically, with regard to the whole, we have every reason to despise, and we must despise, all of them. Those who dare not despise the enemy and all that obstructs our advance and are frightened out of their wits by imperialism and reaction, or who succumb before difficulties and setbacks, are ghost-fearing men of the 20th century.

Many of the stories which we have selected describe from a positive angle the courage of men who had no fear of ghosts. In "The Scholar of Changchow," from *Tales of Yi Chien*, the hero is not afraid of monsters of any kind. He puts it well: "Nothing in the world should be feared; but there are men who scare themselves." San-mang in "Ghosts Avoid Chiang San-mang," from *Notes of the Yueh-wei Hermitage*, having heard a story about catching ghosts, went secretly to a graveyard night after night, as eager and ready to catch ghosts as a hunter is to catch foxes and hares; but he never met a ghost. The writer of this story aptly commented: "San-mang was perfectly sure that ghosts could be caught and bound; he despised ghosts in his own mind and his courage was great enough to frighten the ghosts away. That's why ghosts avoided him." The tale "Chen Peng-nien Blows Away the Ghost of a Hanged Woman," from *What Confucius Did Not Talk About*, is a weird and ghastly one. It describes the ghost of a hanged woman which "stood erect and blew its breath at Chen. The gust of wind was icy cold. Chen's hair stood on end and his teeth chattered, while the lamp turned pale and was on the point of going out." But the next paragraph is full of meaning. Chen Peng-nien then says to himself: "So even ghosts have breath! I have breath too, haven't I?" So he takes a deep breath and blows at the ghost which disappears like thin smoke. The ghost in "Chen Tsai-heng," from *Seven Anecdotes of the Golden Bottle*, made this honest confession: "The truth is that ghosts are afraid of men." This more or less sums up the message of all these stories. Shouldn't we show the same spirit towards all the reactionary forces both at home and abroad, to natural and man-made calamities, and to all things which are outwardly terrifying but are actually not to be feared at all? Could it be that they have "breath" while we have none? Could it be, in actual fact, that they don't fear us but that we should fear them? Is it possible that the more we fear "ghosts," the more they will love us? That they will show mercy and not harm us? And that suddenly all will go swimmingly for our cause, and

7

everything will be bright and rosy, like the flowers that bloom in the spring?

Some of the other stories also show the same fearless spirit and are written in a most interesting manner. One such example is "Juan Teh-ju" from *Records of Light and Dark* of the Southern and Northern Dynasties. Juan sees a ghost in the privy. Unruffled, he says with a smile: "People say that ghosts are hideous; they certainly are!" Thoroughly ashamed of itself, the ghost makes off. This story is terse and amusing. In "What Tsao Chu-hsu Says," also from *Notes of the Yueh-wei Hermitage*, a man who has no fear of ghosts sees a ghost; it tries to frighten him with the dishevelled hair and protruding tongue of the ghost of a hanged person. He smiles at the apparition and says: "It is still hair, only rather dishevelled; it is still a tongue, only a bit longer. What's there to be afraid of?" The ghost then takes off its head and puts it on the table. Still smiling, the man says: "I do not fear you with your head on, so what's there to fear with your head off!" The ghost is thoroughly discomfited. In the story about Keng Chu-ping from "Ching Feng" in *Strange Tales of Liao Chai*, the way one ghost is handled is even more remarkable:

So he (Keng Chu-ping) went alone and read books downstairs. As he sat at the table after dusk, a ghost with matted hair appeared. Its face was as black as charcoal, and it stared at him with bulging eyes. Chu-ping laughed, dipped his finger in the ink and, after smearing it over his face, stared back at the ghost with gleaming eyes. Abashed, the ghost fled.

Reactionary forces both at home and abroad are even more shameless than ghosts. It is sometimes necessary 'or us to use Keng Chu-ping's method, that is: pay them)ack in their own coin! Not that we want to make them ashamed of themselves, but it will put them into a hopeless situation and force them to retreat in face of difficulties.

The thesis that "all reactionaries are paper tigers," put forward by Comrade Mao Tsetung during the Third Revolutionary Civil War period, has armed the people of our country ideologically, strengthened their confidence in victory and played an exceedingly great role in the People's Liberation War. In the struggle against imperialism and for world peace in the coming days, and in the great struggle to overcome finally the remnant forces of the reactionary classes within the country and successfully build a great socialist country, Comrade Mao Tsetung's concept of strategically despising the enemy will continue to inspire us and will also enable us to go on winning great victories. Comrade Mao Tsetung's concept of strategically despising the enemy is always spoken of together with his concept of tactically taking the enemy seriously. As early as 1936, in his *Problems of Strategy in China's Revolutionary War* he said: "Our strategy is 'pit one against ten' and our tactics are 'pit ten against one' — this is one of our fundamental principles for gaining mastery over the enemy."[1] In his article "On Some Important Problems of the Party's Present Policy" written in 1948, he explained in still greater detail that, strategically, with regard to the whole, we should take the enemy lightly and oppose overestimating the enemy's strength. But,

[1] *Selected Works of Mao Tsetung*, Foreign Languages Press, Peking, 1967, Vol. I, p. 237.

with regard to each part, each specific struggle, we must never take the enemy lightly, we must, on the contrary, take him seriously. He said:

If, with regard to the whole, we overestimate the strength of our enemy and hence do not dare to overthrow him and do not dare to win victory, we shall be committing a Right opportunist error. If, with regard to each part, each specific problem, we are not prudent, do not carefully study and perfect the art of struggle, do not concentrate all our strength for battle and do not pay attention to winning over all the allies that should be won over (middle peasants, small independent craftsmen and traders, the middle bourgeoisie, students, teachers, professors and ordinary intellectuals, ordinary government employees, professionals and enlightened gentry), we shall be committing a "Left" opportunist error.[1]

This concept of Comrade Mao Tsetung is a summing up of experience which has stood repeated tests over the long years of China's revolutionary struggle. In these terse terms he elucidates extremely complex questions of revolutionary strategy and tactics, and gives us a fundamental guiding principle for our revolutionary struggle. This is a Marxist-Leninist theoretical generalization of great profundity.

Why should we strategically despise the enemy while tactically taking him seriously? Comrade Mao Tsetung gave a thorough explanation of this at a meeting of the Political Bureau of the Central Committee of the Com-

---

[1] "On Some Important Problems of the Party's Present Policy," *Selected Works of Mao Tsetung,* Foreign Languages Press, Peking, 1961, Vol. IV, pp. 181-82.

munist Party of China held at Wuchang in December 1958. He pointed out that there is not a single thing in the world which is not a unity of opposites, which is without a dual nature. Imperialism and all reactionaries also have a dual nature — they are real tigers and paper tigers at the same time. Looked at in essence, from a long-term point of view, they are paper tigers, and hence we should despise them strategically. In view of the fact that they have eaten millions and tens of millions of people and will continue to eat people in the future, they are real tigers, and we should, therefore, also take them seriously tactically.[1] This shows that the dialectics of our revolutionary theory, the dialectics of our strategy and tactics, are precisely a correct reflection of the dialectics of objective reality. And it is precisely because our theory, strategy and tactics correctly reflect the laws of objective reality that we are able to win every battle we fight. Just as in dealing with the enemy, we must also strategically despise difficulties or setbacks in our work while tactically taking them seriously. Difficulties and setbacks in all revolutionary work are only transient phenomena, merely obstacles or twists and turns in our path of advance; they can be surmounted or overturned. Under certain definite conditions and through conflict, things are always changing positions with their opposites and transforming themselves into their opposites. To people engaged in the stupendous cause of revolution, difficulties and setbacks in revolutionary work are very small things. In this respect, we have every reason to despise

---

[1] See the editorial note of "Talk with the American Correspondent Anna Louise Strong," *Selected Works of Mao Tsetung*, Foreign Languages Press, Peking, 1961, Vol. IV, pp. 98-99.

them. But we must also face up to them, study them seriously and draw the necessary experience and lessons from them, find effective measures to overcome or overturn them, and resolutely carry these measures through so as to conquer them and move ahead successfully. So in this respect we should also take them seriously.

In these stories about not being afraid of ghosts, which we have selected, the stress is put on men's courage, their fearlessness towards ghosts and monsters and their bravery in striking at them, so, perhaps a greater emphasis has been put on the spirit of strategically despising the enemy. But some of these stories may serve to illustrate the need to combine closely the idea of strategically despising the enemy with that of tactically taking him seriously. The first story in this booklet, "Sung Ting-po Catches a Ghost," from the *Tales of Strange Things*, is very interesting and meaningful. The man in the story, who dared to catch ghosts even when a youngster, was not only brave but prudent. He showed no fear at all when, walking out one night, he met a ghost; mentally he completely held the initiative. Besides, he was clever at doing what was appropriate to the specific situation so as to keep the ghost under his control from start to finish. First, the ghost asked him who he was. He put the ghost off its guard by saying: "I am a ghost too." The ghost then suggested that they carry each other pick-a-back by turn. When it discovered he was very heavy, the ghost began to have doubts. Once again he quieted its suspicions, saying: "I am a new ghost. That's why I am heavy." When they came to a river, the ghost waded noiselessly while he splashed through; the ghost got suspicious again.

"How comes it that you make such a noise?" asked the ghost. He threw it off its guard for a third time by saying: "That's because I am a new ghost, I am not accustomed yet to wading through water. You mustn't blame me." He not only succeeded in misleading the ghost with false phenomena from start to finish but also learned from it how ghosts could be subdued. He said that, as a new ghost, he would like to know what ghosts were afraid of. Said the ghost: "What we detest is men's spittle." Later when the ghost transformed itself into a sheep, he spat on it to prevent it from transforming itself again and getting away. And so he finally caught the ghost. Doesn't this story show exactly that this ghost-catching man not only mentally despised the ghost on the whole but was extremely cautious and resourceful in his actual dealings with the ghost?

A similar story is "Black Magic" from *Strange Tales of Liao Chai*. In this story, a certain Mr. Yu did not believe a fortune-teller in the street who told him that he would die in three days. He refused to let himself be blackmailed. However, he did not fail to keep a vigilant lookout when he got back to his inn. On the third day, he sat quietly in his room waiting to see what would happen. The day passed uneventfully. At nightfall, he shut his door, lit the lamp and, with a sword at his side, sat waiting expectantly. The fortune-teller, who had magic powers, sent a "little man" with a spear to kill him. The man seized his sword, cut the "little man" right through the middle, and found that it was made of paper. Later, a hideous hobgoblin appeared. He cut it with his sword, and found it was made of clay. After some time, a giant devil standing as tall as the eaves of the house came. When it pushed at the window the walls shook as if they would crumble. Fearing that the house would fall and crush him, Mr. Yu burst open the door and rushed out to fight the devil. Being a skilled fencer, Mr. Yu finally overpowered it and found that it was made of wood. If Mr. Yu had not shown himself to be unafraid of magic powers, ghosts or monsters, and if at the same time he was not fully alert and prepared, arms at hand and skilled at fencing, wouldn't he have been killed by the apparitions and devils sent by the fortune-teller? How otherwise could he shatter the fortune-teller's magic powers and finally give him the punishment he deserved?

There are other tales in this booklet with a similar content, but their plots are not as complex and intricate as those of the two stories mentioned above. So we are not going to deal with them. All of them drive home this truth: On the whole, ghosts are nothing to be afraid of; it is entirely possible for men to defeat and subdue them. But, with regard to each specific ghost and the specific circumstances under which ghosts are handled, it is necessary for men to be prudent and resourceful before they can win final victory. This is a truth with deep meaning. There are no such things as ghosts in the world, but since our ancient legends and superstitions described ghosts as something that could harm men, the writers of these tales created their stories on the basis of the experience men had gained in real life and of the experience men had acquired in their struggle against harmful things, and so brought forth this truth. Of course, had it not been for Comrade Mao Tsetung's profound theoretical generalizations and the guidance of his teachings, it would not be so easy for us to see the meaning and moral of these stories.

As early as 41 years ago, when devils held sway in China and demons were rampant, the *Hsiangkiang Review*, edited by Comrade Mao Tsetung, in its first issue sent out the call to the Chinese people:

What should you not fear? Do not fear the heavens, do not fear ghosts, do not fear death, do not fear the bureaucrats, warlords, or capitalists.

How inspiring is this dauntless spirit! All Marxists and all the revolutionary people who take upon themselves the task of transforming the world should have this lofty spirit and revolutionary mettle; they should thoroughly do away with superstitions, emancipate their minds and be tough-willed men who fear nothing at all, who are both resourceful and bold, with both heaven-storming drive and the scientific analytical spirit.

The Institute of Literature of the Chinese Academy of Social Sciences started compiling this book in the spring of 1959 when, all over the world, imperialism, the reactionaries in various countries and the revisionists organized a big anti-China chorus; by the summer of that year the compilation was basically completed. That was the time when revisionists inside the country rose in response to international revisionism and launched their frenzied attack against the leadership of the Party. We decided then to make a further careful selection from the first manuscript and enrich its content; it was also decided that I should write a preface.

There are plenty of devils, ghosts and goblins in the world, and it will take some time to wipe them out. Within the country, too, there are still great difficulties;

the remnants of the devils in Chinese shape are still making trouble; and there are still many obstacles to overcome in the path of our great socialist construction. It seems very necessary, therefore, to publish this book. After the Ninth Plenary Session of the Eighth Central Committee of the Communist Party of China formulated in January 1961 the policies to be followed in the domestic political, economic and ideological fields, and since more people have come to understand the strategy and tactics of revolutionary struggle under present conditions, publication of this book of *Stories About Not Being Afraid of Ghosts* may not come as such a big surprise to the public.

January 23, 1961

Sung Ting-po Catches a Ghost

Sung Ting-po of Nanyang, when a young man, met a ghost one night as he was walking.

"Who are you?" he asked.

The ghost answered, "A ghost." It then asked, "And who are you?"

"I am ghost too," lied Sung.

"Where are you going?"

"To the town of Wan," was the reply.

"So am I."

They went along together for several *li*.

"Walking like this is too slow. Why not carry each other in turn?" suggested the ghost.

"A good idea," agreed Sung.

First the ghost carried him for several *li*.

"How heavy you are!" said the ghost. "Are you really a phantom?"

"I am a new ghost," answered Sung. "That's why I am heavy."

Then he carried the ghost, who was no weight at all. And so they went on, changing several times.

"As I am a new ghost," remarked Sung presently, "I don't know what we spectres have to fear most."

"What we detest is men's spittle."

They proceeded together till they came to a stream. Sung invited the ghost to cross first, which it did without a sound. Sung, however, made quite a splash. "How comes it that you make such a noise?" inquired the ghost.

"That's because I am a new ghost. I am not accustomed yet to wading through water. You mustn't blame me."

As they approached the town of Wan, Sung threw the ghost over his shoulder and held it fast. With a screech the ghost begged to be put down, but Sung paid no attention, making straight for the town. When he set the ghost down, it had turned into a sheep. He promptly sold it, having spat at it first to prevent it from changing into another form. Then he left, the richer by one thousand five hundred coins.

Shih Chung[1] commented on this at the time as follows:

Sung Ting-po did better than most,
Made fifteen hundred coins by selling a ghost.

(From Tales of Strange Things by an author of the Wei or Tsin Dynasty)

---

[1] A wealthy nobleman in the Tsin Dynasty. The author of this tale used his name to prove that this was a true story.

宋定伯捉鬼

Sung Ting-po Catches a Ghost

Juan Teh-ju

Once in the privy Juan Teh-ju saw a ghost. More than ten feet tall, black with bulging eyes, it was dressed in a dark coat and cap. And this apparition was less than a foot from his side. Quite calm and composed, Juan told it with a smile: "People say that ghosts are hideous; they certainly are!" Then, red with shame, the ghost made off.

(From *Records of Light and Dark* by Liu Yi-ching of the Southern and Northern Dynasties)

Tsui Min-chueh

Tsui Min-chueh of Poling was an honest lad who feared neither gods nor devils. When he was ten sudden illness carried him off, but eighteen years later he came to life again. He related that he had been taken by mistake, but after one year by dint of hard argument had obtained his release.

The king of hell said, "You should be sent back by rights. But since your corpse has rotted away, how can you return to it?"

Still Tsui pleaded to be sent back.

"You can be reborn as an infant," said the king. "And we shall grant you double official honours."

Tsui still refused, however.

Unable to refute him, the king was in a quandary for a long time. So when Tsui demanded that his wrong be righted, the king was forced to send to the western regions for a life-restoring drug. After several years the messenger returned with the medicine, which was smeared on the skeleton; and soon flesh covered all except the soles of the feet, where the bones still showed.

Then Tsui appeared to his family repeatedly in dreams and said, "I have come back to life."

They opened the coffin, found him breathing, and in

a month or more nursed him back to health. While in the nether regions Tsui had looked up the records and, having learned that he would serve as prefect ten times, he sought out posts which were reputed unlucky and treated the ghosts and spirits there with contempt. And no ill ever befell him.

Some time later he was appointed Prefect of Hsuchow. His predecessors had never dared to stay in the main hall, for tradition had it that this was the old residence of Hsiang Yu. Tsui gave orders on his arrival to have the hall cleared for the transaction of business. After a few days, he heard a loud shouting in mid-air, "I am the Conqueror of Western Chu! Who is Tsui Min-chueh that he dares to move into my house?"

Tsui remarked calmly, "What a scoundrel this Hsiang Yu is! In his life he failed to win the kingdom in the west from the First Emperor of Han. Now after death he is disputing with me over a tumble-down house. He killed himself at Wuchiang and his head was carted ten thousand *li* away. Even if he manages to haunt this place, there is nothing to be afraid of."

Then utter silence fell, and the hall ceased to be haunted.

Still later, when Tsui served as Prefect of Huachow, early one night a man near the shrine of the god of Mount Hua heard a tumult in the temple. Going to look, he saw a great display of torches and several hundred soldiers drawn up to await orders; then someone announced that they were there to welcome the bride of the god's third son, and they were told, "Prefect

Tsui is in this district. Mind you don't bring high winds and torrential rain."

"We would not dare!" they answered. With that they trooped out and vanished.

(From *A Wide Survey of Marvels* by Tai Fu of the Tang Dynasty)

Tou Pu-yi

Tou Pu-yi, the grandson of a famous minister of the Wu Teh Era,[1] served as captain of the imperial guard before retiring on account of old age. He went home to Taiyuan where he had a house in Yangchu County north of the city.

Tou was brave and completely fearless, and had done many chivalrous deeds as a young man. He often gathered a dozen or so companions for cock-fights and hunting with hounds. They would stake tens of thousands of cash on one throw of the dice, and tried to see which could outdo the rest in daring. A few *li* northeast of Taiyuan the highway was haunted by a ghost twenty feet tall, which often came out in the dark or on rainy days to frighten people to death.

The young fellows said, "We'll give five thousand cash to the man who will go and shoot this ghost!"

The others kept silent, but Tou volunteered to go. He set out that very evening.

The others said, "When he gets out of the city he may go into hiding and come back tonight pretending to have shot the ghost. How can we trust him? Let's follow him secretly."

Tou reached the ghost's hide-out just as the ghost

---

[1] 618-626 A.D.

was emerging. He gave chase and drew his bow, and the ghost fled, transfixed by his arrow. Tou ran after it and pierced the ghost with three arrows till it plunged over the cliff. Then he started back and the others came to meet him, laughing.

"We were afraid you would hide and try to trick us," they said. "So we followed you secretly. Now we know how bold you are!" They gave him the money, which Tou spent all on wine.

The next day he went to the cliff where he had shot the ghost and found a funeral effigy made of woven wicker. (In the capital such figures are made of bamboo, but since there is none in Taiyuan they use wicker instead.) He found his three arrows beside it. That was the end of this highway ghost. And that is how Tou won a name for courage. When he retired aged more than seventy, he still had all his early spirit.

(From *Hearsay Tales* by Niu
Su of the Tang Dynasty)

Chen Luan-feng

During the Yuan Ho Era[1] in the Tang Dynasty, there lived a certain Chen Luan-feng in Haikang County. Confident in his strength and uprightness, he feared neither ghosts nor deities; and his fellow countrymen called him "Chou Chu the Second."[2]

Now the people of Haikang used to sacrifice reverently in the temple of the god of thunder; there was so much praying and worshipping that some unholy manifestations were caused by it. Every year when thunder first sounded, the people would remember the cyclical sign of the day; and when another day with the same cyclical sign came round, work of every kind had to stop. Those who broke this rule were struck by thunderbolts within a couple of days — this came to pass as surely as an echo follows a sound.

One year there was a serious drought in Haikang and they prayed to the god in vain. In a towering rage, Chen cried, "Our district is the home of thunder. Yet the thunder god will not help us after taking all these offerings and libations! Now the crops have withered,

---

[1] 806-820 A.D.

[2] A brave, hot-tempered man in the Tsin Dynasty. The local people, who were plagued by a tiger and a great serpent, called these and Chou Chu their Three Evils. But later Chou Chu killed the tiger and serpent and mended his ways.

the pools are dry and all our cattle have been sacrificed. What use is this temple?" He took a torch and set fire to it.

It was commonly believed there that a man who ate yellow croaker and pork together would be killed by a thunderbolt too. But today Chen went out to the fields with a chopper and ate the tabooed food together to see what would happen. Sure enough, strange clouds appeared, a fierce wind blew up, crashing thunder and torrential rain struck at him. Chen swung his chopper over his head and chopped at the thunder god's left leg so that it fell to the ground. It was blue in colour and had the form of a bear or pig with hairy horns and fleshy wings, while in its hand was a short-handled stone axe. As it wallowed in blood the clouds and rain disappeared. Knowing that the thunder god was powerless, Chen ran home to tell his kinsmen, "I have chopped off Thunder's leg! Come and have a look."

In consternation, his relatives went to see this, and found the thunder god with its leg broken. Chen raised his chopper and was about to cut the creature's throat and bite it, but he was stopped by the crowd.

"Thunder is something divine from heaven, while you are a common mortal on earth," they said. "If you kill the thunder god our whole district is sure to suffer for it."

They grabbed hold of his clothes so that Chen could not attack it. Meanwhile clouds and thunder came down again to enfold the wounded god and carry it off with its severed leg. After that there was a downpour of rain from noon till dusk, so that all the parched shoots revived. Then old and young upbraided Chen and forbade him to return to his house. Chopper in

Sung Ting-po Catches a Ghost

hand, he walked for some twenty *li* to the house of a cousin. That night another thunderbolt struck, destroying the room where he was with fire from heaven. Once more he stood in the courtyard with his chopper, and the thunder could not harm him. Then someone told his cousin what had happened, and he was driven out again. He went to a monastery, but a thunderbolt struck and burned the place as before. Chen knew that no one else would take him in, so he went with a torch by night to a cave with stalactites, where no thunderbolt could strike him. And there he stayed for three nights before going home.

After this, whenever there was a drought in Haikang, the people would collect money for Chen and ask him to prepare the forbidden food and eat it, taking his chopper as he had done before. And every time there would be a downpour of rain, but no thunderbolt could strike him. So it went on for more than twenty years, and folk called him the Master of Rain.

During the Tai Ho Era[1] the Prefect Lin Hsu heard of this and summoned Chen to his office to ask for an account of what had happened.

Chen said, "When I was young and strong, my heart was like stone or iron — I cared nothing for ghosts or deities, thunder or lightning. Because I was willing to give my life to save the people, Heaven could not let the thunder demon have its wicked way." He presented his chopper to the prefect, who rewarded him handsomely.

(From *Strange Tales* by Pei Hsing of the Tang Dynasty)

---

[1] 827-835 A.D.

Wei Pang

During the Ta Li Era[1] in the Tang Dynasty, there was a scholar named Wei Pang who possessed unusual strength and who travelled at night without fear. He was a good horseman and archer, and never left home without his bow and arrows. He not only cooked all the birds and beasts he caught, but even ate whatever snakes, scorpions, earthworms, dung beetles, mole-crickets and the like he found.

He was out at dusk once in the capital when the sounding of the evening drum surprised him still far from his destination, and he did not know where he could find a lodging. Then he noticed a respectable-looking family in that neighbourhood moving out of their house and about to lock the gate. Wei asked if he might spend the night there.

The master of the house said, "There is a dead man next door. As the saying goes, this house is under the influence of an evil spirit. If anyone goes in, he will be hurt. So we are moving to a relative's house near by to keep out of harm's way till tomorrow. I cannot conceal this from you."

"Just let me stay here for the night," said Wei. "You

---

[1] 766-779 A.D.

Chen Luan-feng

need not worry about anything. If there is an evil spirit, I shall bear the brunt of it."

The owner of the house led him inside, opened up the hall and kitchen and showed him where a bed, food and drink were to be had. Wei told his servant to stable his horse and light a candle in the hall, then prepare a meal in the kitchen. After eating, he made his man sleep in another room while he put his couch in the hall and opened the door. Then he blew out the candle, held his bow ready, and sat there to wait for the ghost.

Towards the end of the third watch, a bright object resembling a large disc, shining like fire, flew down from the air to the door. When Wei saw this he was delighted. Drawing his bow-string to the full in the dark, he let fly an arrow which hit the target in the centre. There was a crackling and flames darted out. He shot three times in succession, till the light grew dim and the thing ceased to move. Bow in hand, he went to pull the arrows out. Thereupon the shining object fell to the ground. Wei called his servant to fetch a light and found that this was a lump of flesh with eyes all over it. When these eyes flickered they emitted sparkling gleams. Wei said with a laugh, "So the master of the house was right when he said that this place was under the influence of an evil spirit!" And he told his man to cook it. The meat smelled most appetizing. Well cooked and chopped into a mince, it tasted quite delicious. He shared it with his servant, leaving half to show the master of the house. At dawn when the latter came back, he was pleased to find Wei safe. And when Wei told him how he had killed the ghost and presented the meat he had kept, the owner of the house was greatly amazed.

(From *Tracing the Changes* by Huangfu of the Tang Dynasty)

The House of Lord Shih

Liu Yung, Assistant Master of the Imperial Kitchen, who used to visit Loyang when a young man, once told ne that south of Tientsin Bridge[1] there was a house known as the House of Lord Shih, which being reputedly haunted had remained uninhabited for nearly thirty years. This house was complete with pools, bamboo groves, pavilions, kiosks, flowers, trees and studies, and every spring groups of pleasure-seekers would come, bringing wine, food and musical instruments, to enjoy themselves there. In fact it was one of the sights of Loyang.

During the Tuan Kung Era,[2] there was a good drinker called Chu, an irascible man and something of a bully. One day some young fellows invited him to go there and said, "You know this is a haunted house. We will treat you to enough drinks to make you tipsy if you can spend a night here."

"This is a scheme after my own heart," said Chu. "Most men fear death, but not I. So why should I be afraid of a haunted house?"

· The young men approved and had the hall swept clean and a couch set for him there before they left.

---

1 A bridge over the River Lo at Loyang.
2 988-989 A.D.

Soon Chu was sound asleep on the couch. This was the first month of summer, the porch was filled with faint shadows of bamboos and trees rustled in the breeze while moonlight flooded in. Suddenly he was aroused and saw the doors of the pavilions in both wings open one after the other, and out from each stepped a young maid with a lamp. Having placed these on the steps they turned and withdrew. Soon several splendidly costumed women appeared and sat down by the lamps to sew. As Chu watched in astonishment, the door of the back hall was flung open, and all manner of utensils, couches and curtains were brought in; after which maids with candles in their hands led out two ladies dressed with magnificent taste, who were carrying polosticks. They announced, "The master has arrived." But the sight of Chu was a shock to them. "Wait!" they cried.

Then a man in a tall hat and military costume sat on the couch and shouted at the women: "This fellow must be a thief! Have him thrown out!" In no time the ladies had reached Chu's couch, lifted him bodily and tossed him into the bamboo grove west of the hall. The dry branches tore his flesh and made him bleed. In a rage Chu picked himself up and marched straight back to the hall. Wagging a finger at the man, he swore, "In your life you stole high position, you time-server; after death you have stolen a house and are still making trouble. Yet you have the effrontery to call me a thief!" With that he seized a cushion and threw it at the man, hitting him on the shoulder. They all scattered in panic, disappearing in no time.

Wei Pang

It was then the fifth watch,[1] and the young men burst through the gate carrying flaming torches. Amazed to find Chu unharmed, they asked what had happened, and Chu told them the whole story, showing where he had been injured by the dry branches. Then they all admired his courage.

(From *Chats at Friendly Gatherings* by Shangkuan Yung of the Sung Dynasty)

---

[1] Just before dawn.

Wang Chih-fu

Wang Chih-fu of Laiwu in Yenchou, though he came of peasant stock, was a man of firm principles who would not pander to ghosts or deities. If his wife or children fell ill he nursed them as best he could, but would never consult spirits or exorcists. When his relatives and friends urged such a course, he replied, " 'Life and death are decreed by fate, rank and riches determined by Heaven.' Don't ask me to alter the convictions of a life-time."

In the spring of the first year of the Chen Lung Era[1] of the Kin Dynasty, strange apparitions were seen and ghosts appeared in Wang's courtyard at noon. They peeped through doors, screeched from the rafters, moved beds and cooking vessels, sang, laughed and ran about playing tricks of every kind. The whole household could hardly sleep or eat for fear. Wang alone remained unperturbed, and summoning old and young he urged them, "Don't be afraid because these are strange creatures. We are men, created in the form of the universe with true light in our nature. These creatures are spectres of darkness. What can darkness do to light? Keep calm and don't show undue alarm or anxiety." Then his family regained confidence a little.

---

[1] 1156-1161 A.D.

One day as Wang was seated in the hall, a huge demon seven feet tall appeared in a high hat, broad belt, long gown and crimson shoes. This spectre bowed to him. When Wang did not change colour, the demon straightened its dress respectfully and said, "Now, you are indeed a true man! We admire you profoundly! Thinking your stern appearance might hide a timid heart, we resorted to various strange antics to try you; yet you seemed neither to have heard nor seen us. We shall not dare repeat this performance." With another respectful bow the demon vanished.

(From *Tales of Yi Chien* by Hung Mai of the Sung Dynasty)

Chiang Chien

Chiang Chien, who styled himself the Seeker After Knowledge, was a native of Fengfu in Yenchou. His home was in the county town a hundred *li* from where he studied. Whenever he went back to see his father, he would set out just as the fancy took him, regardless of whether it was morning or night. He was riding along once at midnight with his bow and arrows at his waist, when the servant boy in front saw gleams of light in the forest and was too frightened to go on.

Chiang said, "These are simply ghosts. Why should we be afraid?" Riding nearer, he saw a dozen men or so with loosened hair, sitting gambling on the ground. He drew his bow and shot at them, whereupon they scattered in alarm and vanished. Several hundred strings of cash were piled on the ground, and he knew this must be paper money. He flicked it with his whip, and it crumbled into ashes. All that was left was a large green stone bowl for dice, translucent and lovely. And this he kept.

(From *Tales of Yi Chien* by Hung Mai of the Sung Dynasty)

The Scholar of Changchow

There was a scholar of Changchow who prided himself on his courage and claimed that nothing in the
world should be feared; but there are men who scare
themselves. He was always regretting that no ghosts
or spirits would challenge him to try out his courage.

One day he went out with a few friends to a village,
where they saw something in a fine silk wrapper on the
ground, and none of the others dared even to look at
it.

"I am hard up," said he with a laugh. "Why
shouldn't I take it?"

He unwrapped it in front of them, and after unrolling
several bolts of silk he found three large ingots of silver
and a magic creature something like a frog. He invok-
ed it, saying, "Begone, evil thing! All I want is the
silver and the silk."

When he took his find home, his family wept bitterly
and prophesied, "Any day now trouble will come."

"I'll take the blame," he said. "You won't be in-
volved."

That night when he went to bed, he found two green
frogs as large as year-old babies on his mat. He had
just been wishing for something to go with his wine, so
he killed them with a club. His family lamented again,
but he cheerfully cut up and cooked the frogs, and hav-

ing eaten them went tipsy to bed to pass a peaceful night. The next night he was visited by a dozen frogs, smaller than the first, and he cooked these too. The next night thirty appeared. Night by night the number increased but the size diminished, until finally his room was filled with frogs and he could not eat them all. So he hired a workman to bury them in the country, becoming even more emboldened. This went on for a month, then the visitations stopped. The scholar laughed heartily. "So that's all the magic creature can do!" he scoffed.

His wife urged him to buy some hedgehogs to catch and eat the frogs if they reappeared. But he said, "I am as good as any hedgehog. What more do we want?" After this his family had no further trouble, and all who knew him admired him.

(From Tales of Yi Chien by
Hung Mai of the Sung Dynasty)

Men Take Refuge from Ghosts in a Bath-house

Hunchback Bridge in Hangchow is commonly said to be haunted by evil spirits which molest passers-by. East of the bridge stands a bath-house with hot water during the night. One day a man walking alone was caught in the rain. Suddenly he found someone else sharing his umbrella and he suspected that this was a ghost. Since they were on the bridge, he pushed the other into the water and took to his heels. Catching sight of a light in the bath-house, he went in to escape from the ghost.

Soon a man came in, drenched, who panted, "A ghost with an umbrella just pushed me into the river so that I was nearly drowned."

When they talked together, each discovered his mistake.

Another man was out walking one night with no lantern when it was drizzling. Hearing footsteps behind him, he turned and saw a huge head on a body only about two feet tall. He stood still to watch, and the big head stood still too. He walked on, and so did the head. He broke into a run, and the head ran too. In fear and trembling he bolted to the bath-house, pushed open the door and dashed in. But before he could close the door the head followed him in, nearly frightening the fellow out of his wits. When he picked up a candle for a better look, it was only a child with a big peck measure on his head to keep off the rain. Because the child was afraid of ghosts too, he had followed closely at his heels. So this man was also mistaken.

Had these four people all gone different ways without clearing the matter up, they would have been convinced that they had seen ghosts. So why should men today think they might see ghosts and be afraid of them?

(From *Anecdotes on Seven Topics* by Lang Ying of the Ming Dynasty)

Su Tung-po and the Wet-nurse

Su Tung-po[1] lived for a while in Pochia Lane outside Changho Gate. (There were two west gates in Kaifeng, the southern one called Yichiu, the northern one Changho.) One day Tai's[2] small son suddenly announced, "There's a thief with a thin dark face, who's dressed in blue."

Su Tung-po told his household to make a search, but no one could be found. Then the wet-nurse went out of her mind, and started behaving and talking as fiercely as a government lictor. When he went to see this for himself, she shouted, "I am the thin, dark one in blue. Not a thief but a ghost. I want this woman to be my witch-doctor."

"I'll let her die sooner than let her leave my house," said Su.

"If you won't let her go, it can't be helped," said the ghost. "But will you have some prayers said for my soul?"

"Certainly not," replied Su.

"Can I have a little wine and food then?" asked the ghost.

"Certainly not," replied Su.

---

[1] A famous poet of the Sung Dynasty.
[2] Su Tung-po's second son.

"How about some paper coins?"

"Certainly not."

"Just a cup of water, please!"

"Give it to her," said Su.

After drinking the water the wet-nurse fell to the ground and came to herself again.

(From *Strange Tales of the Northern Sung Capital* by Li Lien of the Ming Dynasty)

Su Tung-po and the Wet-nurse

Fake Ghosts

When Wang Hai-jih, who used the name Wang Hua, was fourteen years old, he went to study in the monastery on Mount Lungchuan, a place long reputed haunted. Some spirited, self-confident young men from rich families refused to believe this, however. They insulted the monks and moved in to spend a couple of nights there. Then strange things started happening, and quite a few of them were hurt. The monks exaggerated these incidents, till all the rest lost heart and left discomfited. Only young Wang stayed on just as before, and the supernatural happenings ceased.

The monks, surprised by this, pretended to be ghosts to test him. At midnight they would climb to the roof and raise a hullabaloo, drop tiles and stones on his bed, or hammer on his door on stormy nights amid rain, thunder and lightning. But when they peeped through the crack of his door, they saw him sitting up straight with his lamp lit, looking perfectly composed. Although secretly amazed, they redoubled their efforts. After a month they had exhausted their tricks; so when an opportunity came one of them said to him, "During the weird happenings not long ago, many people were injured. How is it that you alone were not afraid?"

"Why should I be afraid?" he retorted.

The monk continued, "After the others left; what else did you see?"

"What should I have seen?" he asked.

"Once you offend a ghost," insisted the monk, "it will reveal its fearful form to overcome you. How could you be the only one to see nothing?"

Wang laughed and said, "I saw some monks haunting the place."

The monks were abashed, imagining that he must have found them out. "Perhaps those monks who died here in time gone by are haunting the place," they suggested.

With another laugh, Wang said, "No. The monks here now."

"You can't have seen us, you must just be guessing," they said.

Wang replied, "I didn't see you, true. But if you didn't do this, how could you tell that I must have seen it?"

Then the monks admitted the truth and made a smiling apology, telling him, "The fact is, we were testing you. You are a man in a thousand. There is no knowing to what heights you will rise."

(From *Anecdotes of the Movable Pavilion* by Chu Kuo-chen of the Ming Dynasty)

The House of Lord Shih

Wang Chieh Is Not Afraid of Ghosts

When I was young I studied in the west suburb, with the birds of the forest as my only neighbours. I would open a book and read from beginning to end before going on to another, never simply dipping into the text or stopping halfway. I would sit up all night without a break, forgetting cold and hunger, not bothering to comb my hair or wash my face.

One night, pen in hand, I was writing an essay when I heard a ghostly screeching outside the window. I reflected that since I had never done any evil, no avenging spirits would come to trouble me, and why should I be afraid of demons or hobgoblins? I lit a torch and went out to track down the sound, which came from a clump of bamboo. I found the wind whistling through the hole in a withered leaf caught on a spider's web, and realized that this was what I had taken for a ghost screeching.

Another night I thought I saw a thief in the side room, and picked up a stick to chase him out. I found a figure standing there erect. When I hit it with the stick, the thief's clothes fell down noiselessly in a heap. I shone a lamp on it, and these were the old servant's clothes which had been washed and hung up there to dry.

So I knew that there were no such things as ghosts — these are simply figments of men's imagination. Since then I have had no more fear.

(From *Wang Chieh's Journal* of the Ching Dynasty)

Black Magic

Mr. Yu in his youth was spirited and gallant, fond of boxing and trials of strength. He was strong enough to raise two heavy bronze vessels and whirl them in the air as fast as wind. During the Chung Chen Era,[1] when he went to the capital for the palace examination, much to his concern his servant fell ill and had to take to his bed. Since there was a fortune-teller in the market-place who was skilled in determining a man's lease of life, Yu decided to consult him. But before he had uttered a word, the fortune-teller asked, "Is it about your servant's illness you want to consult me, sir?"

Much astonished, Yu replied that this was so.

"The sick man will come to no harm," said the fortune-teller. "You, sir, are the one in danger."

Yu thereupon asked to have his own fortune told.

The fortune-teller, having consulted his oracles, told him with a look of horror, "In three days you will be dead."

Yu was struck speechless for some time.

"I know certain small arts," observed the fortune-teller calmly. "Give me ten taels of silver and I will avert this disaster for you."

But to Yu's way of thinking, if his fate was decreed,

---

[1] Reign era of the last Ming emperor, 1628-1643 A.D.

no magic art could change it. So without replying he rose and prepared to leave.

"You begrudge a small outlay," said the fortune-teller. "You'll be sorry for it. You'll be sorry for it!"

All Yu's friends were most concerned and advised him to empty his purse and beg for help, but he would not hear of it. The three days slipped quickly by. Yu sat calmly waiting in his hostel, but nothing happened all day. When night fell, he closed the door and trimmed the lamp to sit there alone with a drawn sword at his side.

As the first watch approached its end and he was unscathed, he was thinking of lying down when he heard a rustling by a crack in the window. A quick look showed him a small creature slipping in armed with a spear, who grew to man's size as soon as its feet touched the ground. Seizing his sword, Yu leaped up and struck at it but missed his adversary, who floated up into the air, shrank back to the size of a midget and made for the crack in the window, hoping to escape. Yu slashed again and felled it with one blow. When he brought the lamp, he found a paper figure cut through the middle. This made him afraid to sleep, and he sat up watching. Presently another creature, ugly and fierce as an ogre, crept through the window. No sooner did it reach the ground than he attacked fiercely, cutting it into two. But since both halves went on twitching and he feared it might come back to life, Yu hacked again and again with his sword, producing a dull thud each time. And when he examined it closely, he found this was a clay image smashed into pieces. So now he moved his seat near to the window and kept his eye fixed on the crack.

After a long time, he heard a noise like an ox wheezing

outside as something pressed against the lattice so hard that the whole house shook and seemed about to fall. To avoid being crushed, Yu decided to go out and fight. He unbolted the door with a clatter and darted out. His eyes fell on a monstrous giant as tall as the eaves. The dim light of the moon revealed its coal-black face and flittering yellow eyes. Stripped to the waist and barefooted, it had a bow in one hand and arrows at its waist. As Yu stared in consternation, the ogre bent its bow. Yu struck the arrow to the ground with his sword; but before he could attack, the ogre took aim again. Yu leaped hastily aside to avoid the shot and the arrow pierced the wall, which clanged and quivered. In a passion, the ogre drew its sabre and whirled it like the wind to smash down on Yu; but the latter darted nimbly forward so that the sabre hit a rock in the yard, cleaving it asunder. Slipping between the ogre's legs, Yu slashed at its ankles, drawing from them a strange clanging. More enraged than ever, the ogre roared like thunder and wheeled round brandishing its sabre again. Once more Yu ducked and darted forward. The sabre swung down to slice off the lower part of his garment, but meanwhile he had reached the ogre's armpit. He belaboured it hard causing the same strange clanging, till the ogre fell and ceased to move. Yu hit out wildly; his blows produced a muffled sound like the beating of a wooden clapper. When he brought the light, he saw it was a life-size wooden figure with a bow and arrows strapped to its waist and a fierce painted face — where his sword had struck there was blood.

Yu sat up till dawn by his lamp, understanding now that these monsters had been sent by the fortune-teller to kill him and thereby manifest his own magic powers. The next day he told this to all his friends and together they went to find the fortune-teller. But the latter, seeing Yu in the distance, suddenly vanished.

Someone said, "This trick of invisibility can be counteracted by the use of dog's blood."

Following this advice, Yu went again, prepared. The fortune-teller made himself invisible as before. But Yu promptly sprinkled the place where the man had been with dog's blood, and there stood the fortune-teller like an ogre, his face all bespattered with dog's blood, his eyes glaring wildly. Yu seized him and handed him over to the authorities, who had him put to death.

(From *Strange Tales of Liao Chai* by Pu Sung-ling of the Ching Dynasty)

Keng Chu-ping

The Kengs of Taiyuan were at one time a noble family with a magnificent mansion. Later their fortunes declined so that half the mansion was left empty and in ruins. Thereupon weird happenings started. Doors would open and shut of themselves, and members of the household were often frightened at night and raised an alarm. The master, greatly perturbed, moved his family elsewhere, leaving an old man there as gatekeeper. After that the place went even more to rack and ruin, and laughter, talk, singing and music could often be heard there.

This Mr. Keng had a nephew Keng Chu-ping, who was unrestrained and irrepressible. He told the old gatekeeper that if he heard or saw anything he should lose no time in reporting it. One night the gateman saw lights flickering upstairs and ran to tell Chu-ping, who decided to have a look and could not be dissuaded from doing so. Since he knew the place well, he found a path through the brambles and made his way in. He went upstairs, but there was nothing amiss there. Making his way further inside, however, he heard chatting. He peeped in and saw two big candles making the room bright as day. A man in the costume of a scholar was sitting there facing south, with a woman opposite him. Both were over forty. Facing east there was a young man of about twenty, and on his right a girl just turned fifteen. Wine

51

and meat were spread on the table and they were sitting round laughing and chatting.

Chu-ping stepped in without warning and cried with a laugh: "Here's an unexpected guest!"

The others fled in alarm, but the elderly man stepped forward to demand: "Who is this breaking into other people's private quarters?"

Chu-ping retorted, "These are our private quarters, but you have taken possession and are drinking here without inviting your host. Isn't that rather stingy?"

The man looked at him closely and said, "No, you're not our host."

"I am Chu-ping, a man of liberal spirit, the owner's nephew."

The other bowed. "I have long known your great reputation." He invited him in and told his family to prepare fresh dishes, but Chu-ping stopped them. Then the man offered him a cup.

Chu-ping said, "We are old neighbours. No one need run away. I hope you will call the others back to drink with us."

The man called, "Hsiao-erh!" and when the young man came in he said, "This is my son." They bowed and sat down, and Chu-ping asked the other's name. He was told, "I am Hu Yi-chun."[1]

Now Chu-ping was exuberant and a good talker, while Hsiao-erh was equally free and easy in his manner. In the course of conversation, each took a fancy to the other. Since Chu-ping was twenty-one, two years older

---

[1] "Hu" in Chinese also means "fox"; this is to say these people were fox-spirits which according to ancient Chinese superstitions often assume human forms.

than Hsiao-erh, he addressed the latter as his younger brother.

The man said, "I hear that one of your ancestors has written a record of the Tushan clan.[1] Do you know it?" When answered in the affirmative, he continued, "I am descended from the Tushan clan. We can trace our genealogy after the Tang Dynasty, but have no record for the five dynasties before. I hope you will instruct us."

Accordingly Chu-ping gave a brief account of how the lady of Tushan had assisted Yu in his task. His speech overflowed with fine phrases and splendid descriptions, so that the man was delighted and said to his son, "We are lucky today to be hearing something quite new to us. Since Master Chu-ping is no outsider, let us ask Mother and Green Phoenix in to listen too, so that they can learn about our ancestors' virtues."

Hsiao-erh disappeared behind the curtain, and presently out came the old woman and the girl. Chu-ping found Green Phoenix so delicate and charming, with such intelligence in her bewitching eyes, that no mortal woman could compare with her. The man, pointing to the woman, said, "This is my wife," and pointing to the girl, "This is Green Phoenix, our niece. She is quite intelligent and can remember whatever she hears or sees. That is why I have called her in to listen."

Having finished his account, Chu-ping went on drinking and staring at the girl, unable to take his eyes off her. And she, conscious of his gaze, lowered her head. When Chu-ping secretly touched her tiny foot with his toe, the

---

[1] According to ancient legend, Yu, the pacifier of floods, went to Tushan and married a fox-spirit there, the lady of Tushan, who assisted Yu in controlling the flood.

girl hastily withdrew her foot but showed no annoyance. He was in raptures and could not contain himself. Beating the table with one hand, he exclaimed, "If a man had a wife like this, he would not change for a kingdom!"

Seeing that he was growing drunk and talking wildly, the woman and girl rose and retired behind the curtain. In disappointment, Chu-ping said goodbye and left, but he could not dismiss Green Phoenix from his mind. The next night he went back and found her fragrance still about the place; but though he waited all night there was not a sound. He went home and talked it over with his wife, proposing that they move into this house, in the hope of meeting the girl again. His wife refused. So he went alone and read books downstairs. As he sat at the table after dusk, a ghost with matted hair appeared. Its face was as black as charcoal, and it stared at him with bulging eyes. Chu-ping laughed, dipped his finger in the ink and, after smearing it over his face, stared back at the ghost with gleaming eyes. Abashed, the ghost fled. . . .

(From "Green Phoenix" in *Strange Tales of Liao Chai* by Pu Sung-ling of the Ching Dynasty)

Catching a Fox and Shooting
at a Ghost

Mr. Li Chu-ming, the son of Magistrate Li Chin-cho of Suining, is a spirited man and utterly fearless. He is the brother-in-law of Mr. Wang Chi-liang of Hsincheng, the owner of a large house with numerous pavilions where many strange things happen. Li went to stay there one summer and took it into his head to spend the night in a certain pavilion where it was cool. When told that this was haunted, he laughed and paid no attention, insisting on having his bed put there. His host, falling in with his wishes, told some servants to spend the night there with him, but he refused, saying that he preferred to sleep alone and had never feared anything in all his life. His host had incense lit in the censer and, having asked where to put the pillow on the bed, blew out the light, closed the door and left.

Li had not been long in bed when he saw in the moonlight the tea-cup on the table start spinning round, neither falling down nor stopping. He swore at it, and with a clang it halted. Then someone plucked out the incense-stick and waved it in the air, making a pattern with the glow. He got up and shouted, "What impudence, you confounded ghost!" Naked as he was, he left his bed to catch the phantom. He groped with his foot under the bed, but found only one shoe. Not waiting to search in the dark, he padded barefoot to strike the place where the incense-stick had danced. Then the incense returned to the censer and all was still again. As he bent down to grope in the dark corners, something which felt like a shoe leaped up to hit him on the cheek; but when he crouched down to look for it he could not find it. Then he opened the door, went downstairs and called a servant to light a candle. Finding nothing at all, however, he went back to bed. The next morning he told several men to search for his shoe; but although they turned mats and shifted beds they could not find it, and his host gave him another pair. Some time later a man looked up and saw a shoe stuck on the rafters. He hooked it down and discovered it was Li's shoe.

Mr. Li was a native of Yitu County, but he stayed for a while in the house of Mr. Sun of Tzuchuan. The house was spacious but all the rooms were empty, and Li used only half of them. A storeyed pavilion by the south courtyard was separated from the other buildings by a wall, and he often noticed the door of this pavilion opening and shutting by itself, but he paid no attention. Once he was chatting with his family in the courtyard, when the pavilion door opened to reveal a small man sitting there facing north. This man, who was not more than three feet tall, was wearing a green robe and white stockings. Though everyone pointed and stared, he did not move. Li said, "This is a fox-spirit!" He snatched up bow and arrows to shoot at the pavilion. The little man, seeing this, sniggered scornfully and vanished. Li seized a sword and mounted the pavilion, cursing as he searched the place; but he had to come back not having seen anything. Then the place stopped being haunted. He lived there for several years and nothing happened to disturb him.

(From *Strange Tales of Liao Chai* by Pu Sung-ling of the Ching Dynasty)

Kao Chung Fights a Sea Monster

Wenteng County in Shantung abuts on the sea, and a monster started appearing in districts along the coast there in the autumn of the twenty-second year of Kang Hsi.[1] The terror-struck local people told stories about it, believing it to be a ghost, and every day towards evening they would close their doors and seal up their windows. After this had gone on for two months, they had no alternative but to report it to the county office.

Kao Chung, the servant of the county magistrate, was a brave man possessed of great strength and he told his master, "Now a sea monster is troubling the people so that whole families cannot live in peace. This is your responsibility, sir, and so it is my business too. Give me a good horse and a sharp lance, and I'll get rid of it." The magistrate agreed to his request and, lance in hand, Kao Chung rode alone to the coast.

A new moon was rising, the smooth sand glistened like snow. He waited till the second watch, when he saw a blue-faced ghost more than ten feet tall, with sharp horns and branching teeth, hairy arms and a scaly back. It was sitting on the beach in front of five cooked chickens and ten bottles of wine, raising its cup in a hand as large as a fan to drink all by itself. Kao Chung galloped

---

[1] 1683 A.D.

Fake Ghosts

straight at it and lunged out with his lance. In panic, the ghost plunged into the sea. Then Kao Chung took its seat, tore up the chicken and drank off the wine, which added to his courage. Presently the sea surged up and the same ghost came riding out from the waves on a monstrous beast. It brandished its sword and attacked him. For a long time they fought. Then Kao Chung seized his chance and pierced its belly with his lance, whereupon the ghost fled and let fall its sword. Kao Chung picked this up and went back to the county office. On the sword were the words "The Swan-Feather Sword." The magistrate gave orders that it be kept in the county armoury. That was the end of the monster by the sea.

(From the sequel to *Miscellaneous Notes* by Niu Hsiu of the Ching Dynasty)

Yeh Lao-to

There was a man called Yeh Lao-to who came from none knows where. He went about bare-headed and bare-footed, wearing a cloth gown winter and summer alike, a bamboo mat in his hand. One day he put up in a hostel in Yangchow; but found it too noisy and wanted to look for some quieter place. The innkeeper, pointing to a room, told him, "That's very quiet, but it's haunted. No one can sleep there."

"Never mind that," said Yeh. He cleaned up the place himself and spread his mat on the ground. At the third watch that night when he was sleeping, the door swung open and there slowly entered a woman with a strip of silk round her neck, her eyes protruding to hang on her cheeks, and her tongue sticking out several feet. She was followed by a headless ghost carrying two heads; then by a ghost who was black all over, whose ears, eyes, mouth and nose seemed blurred; and finally by a ghost with blotchy, swollen limbs and a belly shaped like an enormous gourd able to contain five piculs.

"There's the smell of a live man here!" they cried. "Let's catch him." They searched the room but were unable to approach Yeh. "He's obviously here, yet we can't find him," said one ghost. "What shall we do?"

The bloated ghost said, "The men we catch are those who feel so afraid that their spirit takes flight from their bodies. This man must be a man who has attained the truth. His heart knows no fear and his spirit has not taken flight; so it isn't easy to catch him."

As the ghosts were looking round, Yeh sat up on his mat and pointing to himself with one hand said, "Here I am!"

Then the ghosts fell in terror on their knees, and Yeh questioned them one by one.

The woman, pointing to the other three, said, "This one died in the water, that one in a fire; that one was executed for robbery and murder; and I hanged myself in this room."

"Will you submit yourselves to my will?" asked Yeh. When they assented, he said, "Go and get reborn. Don't haunt this place any more." Then they bowed and went away.

The next morning Yeh related this to the innkeeper. And after that the room was quiet.

(From *What Confucius Did Not Talk About* by Yuan Mei of the Ching Dynasty)

Ghosts Fear Men Who Pit Their Lives Against Them

Vice-minister Chieh has a distant cousin who fears nothing in heaven or on earth and hates all talk of ghosts and supernatural beings. Whenever he is travelling, he likes to lodge in rooms supposed to be haunted. Once he stopped at an inn in Shantung where he was told that the west chamber was haunted. In great delight he opened the door and marched in. He sat there till the second watch, when a tile fell down from the ceiling.

"Are you a ghost?" he cried. "You can't frighten me except by throwing down something not on the roof."

Then a mill-stone was dropped.

"So you are a tough ghost, eh?" he swore. "Well, you can't frighten me except by breaking my desk."

Thereupon a rock came down and smashed half the desk.

Thoroughly enraged, he swore, "You dog of a ghost! The only way to make me afraid of you is by breaking my head!"

He stood up, tossing his cap to the ground, and waited with his head held high. At that there was absolute silence, and this was the end of all supernatural happenings here.

(From *What Confucius Did Not Talk About* by Yuan Mei of the Ching Dynasty)

The Care-free Gentleman

Tsai Wei-kung, a scholar who had passed the provincial examination, once said: "Ghosts have three tricks: enchantment, obstruction and intimidation." When asked to explain this, he told the following tale.

My cousin Lu was a stipendiary scholar[1] of Sungchiang. Exuberant and liberal he styled himself "The Care-free Gentleman." He was passing through a village west of Maohu Lake one day as dusk was falling, when he saw a woman with a powdered face and dark eyebrows hurrying along helter-skelter with a rope. At the sight of Lu, she hid under a great tree, dropping her rope to the ground. When Lu picked it up and looked at it, he found it was a straw rope with a musty smell. He realized that this must be the ghost of some woman who had hanged herself, and pocketing the rope he went straight on. Then the woman came out of the forest to block his way. When he turned left or right, she did the same. Lu knew this was what is commonly called a "ghostly wall." He bore straight on till the ghost, unable to stop him, uttered a loud shriek and changed into a woman with dishevelled hair, pouring with blood. Her tongue lolling out for over a foot, she came leaping at him.

---

[1] A county scholar who received an annual stipend from the local government.

Lu said, "First you pencilled your eyebrows and painted your face to enchant me. Then you barred my way to obstruct me. Now you are looking fierce to frighten me. You've used all your three tricks, but I'm still not afraid. I don't suppose you have any other tricks left to play. Don't you know that I'm called the Care-free Gentleman?"

Then the ghost resumed its earlier form and fell on its knees to say, "I was a woman of the Shih family in the city. I had words with my husband and in a fit of anger hanged myself. Now I've heard that a woman in a family east of Maohu has quarrelled with her husband too; so I'm on my way there to find a substitute.[1] But you've stopped me half way and taken away my rope. I'm really at my wit's end. All I can do is beg you to grant me life again."

Lu asked how this could be done.

"Go and tell the Shih family in the city to perform a religious service for me," it said. "And get some holy monk to chant plenty of incantations for my reincarnation. Then I can be born again."

Lu replied with a laugh, "I am a holy monk. Let me chant my spell of reincarnation for you." Thereupon he chanted:

> *In this wide world*
> *There is no let or hindrance;*
> *Die or come to life again.*
> *Why look for a substitute?*
> *If you want to, go!*

---

[1] It was believed that the ghost of one who had committed suicide must find some other suicide to take its place before it could be reborn in the world of man.

What could be easier?

The ghost, hearing this, saw light. It fell to the ground to kowtow to him, then rushed swiftly away.

Later the local people said, "This was always a troubled place. But after the Care-free Gentleman passed this way, it has stopped being haunted."

(From *What Confucius Did Not Talk About* by Yuan Mei of the Ching Dynasty)

Chen Peng-nien Blows Away
the Ghost of a Hanged Woman

While Chen Peng-nien was still unknown, he was good friends with his fellow countryman Li Fu. One autumn evening he took advantage of the bright moonlight to call on Li for a chat. This Li, who was a poor scholar, said to Chen, "I have asked my wife for some wine but she has none. Just wait a moment while I go out to buy some, and then we can enjoy the moonlight together."

So Chen took up his poems and sat reading while he waited. Presently a tousled-haired woman in blue came along and opened the door, but shrank back at the sight of Chen. Thinking she was some relative of his host who would not come in because a stranger was there, Chen turned in his seat away from her. Then the woman entered with something in her sleeve which she hid by the threshold before hurrying in. Chen, curious to know what it was, went to the door to look. It was a rope, foul-smelling and stained with blood. He realized that this was the ghost of some woman who had hanged herself; and putting the cord inside his boot, he resumed his seat.

In a little while the woman with the tousled hair came out and felt for the rope she had hidden, but could not find it. In anger she rushed up to Chen, crying, "Give that back!"

"Give what back?" Chen demanded.

Instead of answering, she opened her mouth as she stood erect and blew its breath at Chen. The gust of wind was icy cold. Chen's hair stood on end and his teeth chattered, while the lamp turned pale and was on the point of going out.

Chen thought, "So even ghosts have breath! I have breath too, haven't I?" He took a deep breath and blew back, and wherever his breath touched the woman it made a hole, piercing first her belly, then her breast, and finally making away with her head. In a twinkling she had been blown away like thin smoke, never to appear again.

Soon Li, back with the wine, cried out that his wife was hanging by the bed.

"Don't worry," said Chen with a laugh. "I've got the ghost's cord in my boot." He told Li what had happened. And they went in together to revive Mrs. Li, pouring ginger soup down her throat till she came to.

Asked why she had tried to take her own life, she replied, "Poor as we are, my husband is always entertaining guests. He took the only hairpin I had left to buy wine. I was very upset, but with a guest in the house I couldn't make a scene. Then a woman with tousled hair was standing beside me. She said she was a neighbour living to our left, and told me that my husband didn't take the pin because of the guest but to go to a gambling den. That made me even more angry. I thought: 'He won't be back till late and this guest won't go — I can hardly send him packing.' Then the woman with tousled hair made a ring with her hands and said, 'You can pass through this to the realm of Buddha, where you will have joy untold.' But when I tried to get through the ring, her hands would not close tightly enough and it kept breaking. At last she said, 'I'll get my Buddha belt to help you achieve Buddhahood.' She went out to fetch the belt, but didn't come back. I was in some sort of trance when you came to my rescue."

(From *What Confucius Did Not Talk About* by Yuan Mei of the Ching Dynasty)

Wang Chi-ming

Wang Chi-ming of Wuyuan once moved into the Scholar's Mansion at Shangho, formerly the home of his kinsman Wang Po, a metropolitan scholar. During the night of the first day of the fourth month of the thirty-ninth year of Chien Lung,[1] he had a long nightmare from which he woke to find a ghost tall as the room standing by his curtain. Since Wang was a brave man he leaped up to grapple with the ghost. It rushed towards the door, but hurtled by mistake against the wall and seemed stunned. Wang had just seized hold of its waist when a cold gust of wind made the lamp flicker and go out. Unable to see the ghost's face, he could only feel that its hands were icy cold, its waist as thick as a barrel. He wanted to shout for his family, but not a sound could he utter. It was some time before, mustering all his strength, he managed to raise a shout at which his whole household assembled. The ghost by then had shrunk to the size of an infant. When they held a lamp up to it, they found that Wang was holding a roll of tattered silk wadding. Then tiles and bricks rained down outside the window, and Wang's terrified family urged him to let the ghost go.

Wang laughed and said, "This ghostly crew is trying

---

[1] 1774 A.D.

to scare us, but what can they do? If I let it go, it will help the rest to make trouble. We'd better kill this one as a warning to all other ghosts."

So holding the ghost with his left hand, he took a torch from one of his family with his right and burned it. There was a crackling, blood spurted out, and the stench was unbearable. The next morning his neighbours, who had been disturbed, gathered. But they all had to hold their noses because of the stench. Blood as sticky as glue lay more than an inch thick on the ground, and no one knew what manner of ghost this was. Mr. Wang Feng-ting from an illustrious family wrote his poem *Catching the Ghost* to record this incident.

(From *What Confucius Did Not Talk About* by Yuan Mei of the Ching Dynasty)

The Evil Spirit Whose Bluff Was Called

Chen Fu-chu, a scholar of Jenho County, was a stern, upright man. He had a daughter who was religious from childhood, every day reading Taoist scriptures and abstaining from meat, who would shed tears and refuse to eat when marriage was proposed for her. Since Chen found her repugnant, father and daughter saw little of each other.

In her thirties his daughter fell ill and began to rave wildly. "I am Chang Ssu, a cloth merchant of Kiangsi," she said. "In your last life you were a boatman whose boat I hired to go to Szechuan, but you murdered me for my money. You gouged out my eyes and flayed me, then threw my corpse into the river. I have come to demand your life!"

Chen thought: There are plenty of bandits out to steal money, but they are hardly likely to flay their victims. So he asked in which year this had happened.

The answer was, "The eleventh year of Yung Cheng."[1]

At that Chen laughed. "In the eleventh year of Yung Cheng my daughter was already three years old. How, then, could she still be a boatman?"

Then the young woman slapped her own face and said, "You are certainly sharp, Mr. Chen! I've come to the

---
[1] 1733 A.D.

wrong girl. Give me three thousand cash and I will leave her."

Chen retorted angrily, "You are an evil spirit and a blackmailer. I shall beat you with peach twigs.[1] You don't get any money from me!"

Once more the young woman slapped her face and said, "How sharp you are, Mr. Chen! Since you say I am an evil spirit, I shall behave like one and take your daughter's life. I hope you won't be sorry."

"She is an unfilial daughter and I am disgusted with her," answered Chen. "I shall be delighted if you take her with you. But since we are not enemies, yet you dare to blackmail me like this, I assume she must have come to the end of her natural span of life. If you can kill her at once, I shall believe in your power. If she doesn't die for another three days, that will simply be her fate, none of your doing."

After he said that, his daughter sat up with a start, and the ghost stopped speaking through her.

(From *What Confucius Did Not Talk About* by Yuan Mei of the Ching Dynasty)

---

[1] According to an old superstition, ghosts were afraid of the peach tree and could be driven away if whipped with peach twigs.

Frying a Ghost

The provincial scholar Chou Yi-han of Hangchow was a man of high spirit. One very hot summer he went boating on the lake at night with seven or eight companions. When they reached Mount Tingchia, a friend said, "I hear there are many ghosts by the bridge at Chingtzu Monastery. Why don't we go and look for one? It would be fun if we saw a genuine ghost."

All falling in eagerly with this suggestion, they went ashore and walked to the bridge. There they met a man fishing at night with a net, who was just walking off with his catch. Chou recognized the keeper of his family graveyard and said, "Lend us your net. We'll return it tomorrow morning." When the keeper agreed, Chou told his servant to carry it. The others asked what he wanted with a net. He said, "I mean to catch all the ghosts by Mount Nanping in this net." Then they laughed as they went on, following a small unfrequented track up the mountain. The moon was shining as bright as day and in the forest in front they saw a woman in a red coat and white skirt looking up at the moon.

Chou's companions said, "No woman would stay out there so late at night. This must be a ghost. Who dares be our vanguard?"

Chou volunteered and strode forward. When he was half a bowshot from the ghost, there was a cold gust of wind and the woman turned round. Her face was streaming with blood, her eyes were protruding. Chou trembled and could not advance, but called repeatedly, "The net! The net!" Then the rest of them went forward and threw the net. At once the woman vanished. All they found in the net was a stick of dry wood about one foot long. They took this back and knocked up the graveyard keeper to borrow a sharp saw, with which to saw the stick into small pieces — and fresh blood dripped from the wood. Then they bought a container of lamp oil from the fellow and took this to their boat. There they lit a fire, heated the oil and dropped the wood in. Blue smoke flew up and the wood was reduced to charcoal. Upon their return to the city in the morning, they told their friends, "Last night we had a strange adventure — fried a ghost in an oil container!"

(From *What Confucius Did Not Talk About* by Yuan Mei of the Ching Dynasty)

What Tsao Chu-hsu Says

Tsao Chu-hsu, Secretary of the Board of Revenue, re-
ated the following tale. His cousin Tsao, travelling from
Shehsien to Yangchow, stopped at a friend's house on
he way. It was then the hottest time of summer and
ie was invited to take a seat in the library, a spacious,
airy room. So that evening he asked if he might sleep
:here. "This room is haunted," said his friend. "No
one can pass the night here." Tsao insisted, however,
on sleeping in that room.

At midnight there crept slowly in through the crack of
the door something thin as a sheet of paper. Once inside
the room, it expanded little by little to assume a human
form, that of a woman. But this did not intimidate
Tsao. When the ghost let down its hair and put out its
tongue like the ghost of a hanged woman, he simply
laughed and remarked, "It is still hair, only rather dishevelled; it is still a tongue, only a bit longer. What's
there to be afraid of?" Thereupon the ghost took off
its head and put it on the desk. Again Tsao laughed
and said, "I do not fear you with your head on, so what's
there to fear with your head off!" Since the ghost had
no more tricks, it disappeared.

When Tsao stayed in the same place on his homeward
journey, something crept in at the door again at midnight;
but as soon as the ghost showed its head he spat at it

and said: "So this revolting object is back again!" Then the ghost did not enter the room.

This story is rather like that of Chi Kang.[1] A tiger will never devour a drunken man, for the latter known no fear. When a man is afraid, his mind becomes confused and he loses heart, whereupon a ghost can take advantage of him. If he is not afraid, he can keep all his wits about him and remains in good heart. Then no evil spirit can take possession of him. Thus the writer of that tale about Chi Kang says he remained so calm and composed that the ghost slunk away in shame.

(From Notes of the Yueh-wei Hermitage
by Chi Yun of the Ching Dynasty)

---

[1] A famous scholar of the Kingdom of Wei during the Three Kingdoms Period (220-280 A.D.). The story is told in Pei Chi's *Anecdotes*, another collection of tales compiled during the Tsin Dynasty.

Hsu Nan-chin of Nanpi

Mr. Hsu Nan-chin of Nanpi has great courage. While studying in a monastery once, he was sharing a bed with a friend when two torches blazed out from the north wall at midnight. Looking closely, he saw emerging from the wall a man's face as large as a winnowing fan. The two torches were its eyes. His friend shook with fear and nearly died of fright, but he threw his coat over his shoulders and got up slowly remarking, "I was wanting to read but my candle had burned out. It was very good of you to come!" He picked up a book and sat with his back to the creature to read aloud. He had not read many pages, when little by little the light from the eyes faded. Though he knocked on the wall and called out, it did not come back.

Another night he went to the privy followed by a servant boy carrying a candle. Without warning, the same face emerged from the ground to grin at him. The boy dropped the candle and fell flat on the ground, but Hsu picked it up and put it on the spectre's head saying, "My candle has no stand. It was very good of you to come again." When the spectre just looked up at him without moving, Hsu said, "Can't you take yourself somewhere else, instead of coming here? By the sea

there are men who hanker after foul smells.[1] I suppose
you are one of them. Well, I mustn't disappoint you."
He smeared a filthy paper on its mouth. The spectre
belched, uttered frantic roars, and disappeared after
knocking over the candle. And since that day it has
never been seen again.

(From *Notes of the Yueh-wei Hermitage*
by Chi Yun of the Ching Dynasty)

---

[1] *The Annals of Lu Pu-wei* tells of a man who smelt so obnoxious,
owing to a disease, that none of his family could endure his company.
He went to live alone by the sea and there met a man who, fascinated
by his stench, stuck closely to him.

Ghosts Avoid Chiang San-mang

Ghosts Avoid Chiang San-mang

My father Yao-an had the following tale from my great grandfather Jun-sheng. At Chingcheng there lived a certain Chiang San-mang, a bold, pig-headed fellow. One day he heard from someone how Sung Ting-po made money by selling a ghost, and in high delight he exclaimed, "Now I see ghosts can be caught! If I catch a ghost every night and spit at it when it has changed into a sheep, then take it along the next morning to sell to some butcher, I shall have enough to buy wine and meat for the day."

So every night, equipped with a staff and some rope, he prowled quietly round the graveyards like a hunter on the watch for foxes and hares, but not a ghost did he find. Even when he went to places supposed to be haunted and pretended to fall into a drunken sleep to tempt ghosts to approach, still all remained quiet — not an apparition appeared. One night he saw some will-o'-the-wisps in the forest and hastened to the spot. Before he reached it, however, the will-o'-the-wisps made off in different directions, so that once more he went home a disappointed man. When this had gone on for more than a month without his catching anything, he gave up.

This was because a ghost only bullies a man who is afraid. Since Chiang San-mang was perfectly sure that ghosts could be caught and bound, he despised ghosts in his own mind and his courage was great enough to frighten the ghosts away. That's why ghosts avoided him.

(From *Notes of the Yueh-wei Hermitage* by Chi Yun of the Ching Dynasty)

Tien Pu-man

Tien Pu-man

A hired hand named Tien Pu-man lost his way one night and blundered into a graveyard, where he trampled on a skull.

"If you spoil my face, I'll make trouble for you!" threatened the skull.

Tien, blunt and bold, shouted back, "Who told you to get in my way?"

The skull said, "Someone moved me here. I didn't want to get in your way."

Tien shouted again, "Why not make trouble for the man who moved you?"

"His luck is good, so I can't do anything to him."

Tien laughed scornfully. "So you think I'm helpless, eh? You fear the strong and bully the weak — more shame on you!"

Then the skull said with a sob, "Your spirit is strong, too. I daren't do anything to you. I was only making empty threats. In human society people fear the strong and bully the weak, so why blame a ghost for that? If you'll take pity and roll me into a pit, I shall be most grateful."

Tien charged straight past, however. He heard sobbing behind, but nothing else happened whatsoever.

(From *Notes of the Yueh-wei Hermitage* by Chi Yun of the Ching Dynasty)

Smearing the Ghost's Face with Ink

According to Liu Hsiang-wan, an old scholar was staying with one of his relatives when his host's son-in-law, a young rogue, arrived without warning. Since they were incompatible and neither wanted to share a room with the other, the old scholar was moved to another room. For some reason which he could not fathom, the son-in-law looked at him rather oddly and smiled.

This new room seemed quite pleasant and clean, with brushes, ink-stone and books set ready for use. And by lamplight the scholar started writing a letter home. Suddenly beside the lamp there appeared a woman, no great beauty, but possessed of considerable charm. Though the old man knew this was a ghost, he was not afraid. Indicating the lamp he said, "Since you're here, make yourself useful and trim my lamp." Instead the woman put out the light and stepped forward to stand over him. Very angry, the scholar quickly rubbed his fingers in the ink on the ink-stone and slapped the woman's face, smearing both cheeks with ink. "I'll know you by this mark," he said. "Tomorrow I'll find your corpse, cut it up and burn it." Then with a screech the ghost fled.

The next day he related this to his host, who confessed, "A maidservant did die in that room and often appears at night to trouble men. So we only entertain guests there in the daytime. No one has ever spent a night there. Yesterday, however, we had nowhere else to put you; and we thought since you are elderly and a great scholar, the ghost probably would not come. We did not expect it to show itself again." Then the scholar realized why the young man had laughed up his sleeve at him.

This ghost often walked in the moonlight through the courtyard. Later, when some of the household came across it by chance, the ghost would cover its face with its hands and flee. Once they managed to look at it closely, and saw that its face was still smeared with ink.

(From *Notes of the Yueh-wei Hermitage* by Chi Yun of the Ching Dynasty)

A Tale Told by Tai Tung-yuan

Tai Tung-yuan related that when one of his grand-uncles rented an empty, long-deserted house in a quiet lane, he was told that it was haunted. But he retorted sharply, "I'm not afraid!" When night fell, apparitions appeared in the lamplight and nipping vapours pierced him to the bone. Then a huge ghost roared angrily at him, "Still not afraid?"

He answered, "No!"

The ghost took various fearful forms and after a time asked again, "Still not afraid?"

Again he answered, "No!"

Looking slightly more conciliatory, the ghost said, "I don't absolutely have to drive you away, but you shouldn't have boasted like that. If you'll just say 'I'm afraid,' I promise to leave you."

The other lost his temper and retorted, "I'm really not afraid of you, so why should I pretend that I am? As to leaving or not, please yourself."

The ghost repeated its request several times, but met with no response. Then with a great sigh it said, "Thirty years and more I have lived here and never come across such stubbornness. How can I live with such a stupid fool?" With that it vanished.

Some people blamed him, saying, "Fear of ghosts is only natural, nothing shameful. If you had just pretended to be afraid, you could have smoothed things over. Now if both sides keep attacking, how will it end?"

He replied, "A man with great moral strength can banish devils with calm serenity, but that is beyond me. When I resist in spirit, my spirits are high and no ghost can browbeat me. The least compromise, however, would lower my spirits and a ghost would seize its advantage. That ghost was offering me all sorts of bait. I'm lucky not to have fallen into its trap."

And those commenting on this story agreed with him.

(From *Notes of the Yueh-wei Hermitage* by Chi Yun of the Ching Dynasty)

Li Hui-chuan's Story

According to Li Hui-chuan, there was a teacher called Yen, whose personal name I forget. The time for the provincial examination was approaching and one night after his pupils had gone home he was reading by the lamp. A serving-boy in his school, bringing in some tea, suddenly gave a cry and fell to the ground so that the bowl was smashed. With a start Yen got up to have a look, and found a ghost with dishevelled hair and glaring eyes standing before him. Yen said with a chuckle, "There are no such things as ghosts. You must be a cunning thief dressed up like this in the hope of frightening me away. All I have are a pillow and a mat. You had better try somewhere else." When the ghost made no move, Yen said angrily, "Still trying to fool me, eh?" He picked up his ferule to hit it, and it vanished. As Yen looked round and saw no trace left, he mused, "Can there really be ghosts after all?" Then he decided, "The rational soul ascends to heaven, the sentient soul descends underground: that's clear enough. So there can be no ghosts in the world. This must have been a fox-spirit." With that he trimmed the lamp and went on reading aloud. Indeed, this scholar's stubbornness was so uncompromising that the ghost got out of his way. For his unyielding firmness sufficed to defeat it.

I heard of another scholar who saw a ghost one night

as he was pacing the porch. He called to it, "You were a man once. Now that you are a ghost, have you lost all human sense? How can you trespass on someone else's courtyard so late at night, intruding on another man's privacy?" Then that ghost vanished too. This is because the scholar was not afraid, and therefore his spirit was not in any turmoil. Thus the ghost could make no impression on him.

Or take the case of Mr. Shen Feng-kung of Kucheng. (His other name was Ting-hsun and he passed the examination in the same year as my father.) Out walking at night once he was caught in the rain, and the road became so muddy that he and his servant had to support each other; but soon they lost their way. When they came to a ruined monastery which was said to be haunted, Mr. Shen suggested, "Since there's no one to direct us, let's go and ask the way from a ghost." He walked round the balustrade, shouting, "Brother Ghost! Brother Ghost! Tell me, how deep is the water in front?" When there was no answer, he said with a laugh, "I suppose all the ghosts are asleep. I'll take a nap too." So he and his servant leaned against a pillar and slept till morning. This is a case of an easy-going gentleman, just having his bit of fun.

(From *Notes of the Yueh-wei Hermitage* by Chi Yun of the Ching Dynasty)

The Man of Chingho

A certain man of Chingho was riding back on a donkey one night from the city. Passing alone through the countryside, he blundered into a graveyard and lost his way completely. Suddenly someone called his name from behind, but he rode on without looking over his shoulder. Whatever it was behind called more urgently and gave chase; and presently it was on the donkey too, with both hands round his waist, hands cold as ice which would not let go. Since he was a bold man, he pretended not to know that this was a ghost; but secretly taking off his belt he caught it by surprise and strapped it to him. The ghost begged frantically to be released, but he paid no attention, riding quickly back. Reaching his door, he shouted, "I've caught a ghost!" By the time his family came out with torches, he had dismounted and unfastened his belt, and his burden had changed into the rotted plank of a coffin, no longer assuming a human form.

(From *Rambling Notes During Chats at Night* by Ho Pang-eh of the Ching Dynasty)

Pan the Scholar

Pan Yu-yu, a scholar of Huchow Prefecture, was so poor before passing the examination that he never had enough oil for his lamp when studying at night. Often he had to sit alone in the room reciting various classics by heart till late. One day in the depth of winter, just before midnight, he heard a rustling outside. Since there was a little moonlight, he went quietly to the window to have a look. He saw a man with dishevelled hair and curly beard, and a face as black as the Conqueror of Chu in *A Thousand Catties of Gold*.[1] Pan waited silently with bated breath. The man took from his pocket something long and pointed like a chisel. This he pushed through the window lattice to make a square hole, and Pan realized that he meant to reach inside. So having dipped his hands in the basin of water by his desk, when the other thrust his in, Pan seized it with both hands as hard as he could. At first the man struggled, then he became motionless; and soon Pan felt that his wrist was as cold as ice. He let go, and the other fell with a crash down the steps. Amazed at the noise, Pan unbolted the door to find that the man had died, and there was nothing he could do about it.

---

[1] A play by Shen Tsai of the Ming Dynasty about Hsiang Yu the Conqueror of Chu and General Han Hsin. Hsiang Yu in this play has his face painted black.

When day broke, he went to the county office to ask for an examination of the corpse. After the magistrate had conducted a post-mortem, he asked for a detailed account of what had happened, then said with a laugh to Pan, "He wanted to frighten men by disguising himself as a ghost, but instead he was frightened to death himself by a man. He got what he deserved. You had no intention of killing the thief, but were simply paying him back in his own coin. You are not guilty of murder." He ordered the local bailiff to supply a coffin and have the dead man buried. So the case was closed.

(From *Tales to Bury Sorrow* by Chu Yi-ching of the Ching Dynasty)

Chen Tsai-heng

My fellow countryman Chen Tsai-heng is a kindly man with a sense of humour in his sixties. One night he was walking in the open country when he saw two men ahead of him carrying lanterns. He asked for a light for his pipe from one of the lanterns, but try as he might he could not get it lit.

One of the two asked, "Have you passed the first seven days?"[1]

Surprised by this question, Chen answered vaguely, "No."

"No wonder, then," said the other. "Your vital forces aren't yet fully spent. That's why you can't make use of ghostly fire."

Realizing that these two were ghosts, Chen deliberately asked them, "Is it true, as they say, that men are afraid of ghosts?"

The other said, "No. The truth is that ghosts are afraid of men."

"What is there to be afraid of in men?" asked Chen.

"We are afraid of being spat at."

Then Chen drew a deep breath and spat at them. The two ghosts fell back over three steps and glaring angrily at Chen demanded, "Aren't you a ghost?"

---

[1] I.e. the first seven days after death.

With a laugh, Chen answered, "To tell you the truth, I'm a man with one foot in the grave."

He spat at them again, and they shrank to half their size. After he had spat at them three times, the ghosts disappeared.

(From *Seven Anecdotes of the Golden Bottle* by Huang Chun-tsai of the Ching Dynasty)